Magic:

One SMART Horse

By

Jody Lynn McBrien

Photos by

Brendan Makowicz

Dedicated to the staff and riders at SMART

Loving thanks to my children, Katie and Brendan; to Pete, for buying
Mag for me; to Mark; and to one amazing horse, Magic

For more information, contact the author at
canardjl@hotmail.com

TABLE OF CONTENTS

Magic, One SMART Horse

This is a true story. Of course, horses don't talk to each other the way you and I do. But as I have watched Magic interact with other horses over the 10 years that I have owned him, I have seen some remarkable communication, some of which is described in this book. I hope you enjoy getting to know Magic, his horse friends, and the wonderful people at SMART.

Chapter One: News at the Barn

Spanish moss swayed in the gentle breeze on a surprisingly cool August morning. Of course, "cool" means high seventies during a southwest Florida summer. The horses were enjoying the soft wind that helped them keep flies off of their backs and legs. Some dozed in the shade of the wild oak, while other munched quietly on blades of grass. Too soon, autumn and winter would come. Even though the winters are warm in south Florida, the grass stops growing, and the horses dream of spring and sweet new greens in the pasture.

Kaycee, "Mr. K" as he was known by those who cared for him, was happily nibbling on some grass when Tara came and pushed him away. "Why do you pick on me?" Kaycee asked, as he was forced to move or feel Tara's heels kick at his sides.

"Kaycee, you are old! Your coat is dull, and it has gray hair in it. I need the green grass in the shade to keep my soft coat shiny!" Tara replied. It was true: Mr. K was a 22-year old Arabian chestnut whose coat now had many strands of gray. He was a kind and generous horse, though, who was sometimes pushed around by other horses because of his age and his small size.

Reluctantly, Kaycee moved to another place where the shade was losing to the growing daylight. Just then, the noise of a truck bumping over the potholes in the gravel drive sounded its arrival at the barn. The horses pricked up their ears and looked towards the long driveway. They recognized the truck of their beloved caretaker, Samantha, towing the white horse trailer that had brought so many of them to this wonderful place of refuge. Instinctively, Kaycee neighed. In response, an unseen horse whinny came from the trailer. A new arrival!

Chapter Two: The New Arrival

After the horses heard the call of the new horse, their excitement grew, and they began to run around their field, snorting and kicking up their heels. A newcomer to the herd was always cause for both excitement and concern. What would this new horse be like? Would he, or she, change the order of the herd? How would the new horse fit in?

Sam stopped the truck just short of the barn. "Easy!" she called to the herd. "It's okay!" She walked to the side door of the trailer and opened it first, allowing the new horse to take in his new surroundings. "Here we are, Magic," she said. "Good boy. It's okay."

Magic reached his head out the door, and the breeze brought the scent of the horses who would become his new companions. Kaycee called again, and Magic responded. Sam laughed. "Oh, so you've found a new friend already, huh? You know, that might not be such a bad idea…" Sam had been wondering just who to pair this unusual horse with, and the quick connection with "Mr. K" gave her an idea. First, though, to get Magic comfortable in his new stall.

Sam detached Magic's lead rope from where he had been tied in the trailer before opening the back ramp. "Okay, boy," she said, when it was safe for Magic to back out. "Come on out, Mag."

Slowly, Magic backed out of the trailer, and Sam caught his lead rope as he reached the end of the ramp. She patted his neck. "Good boy," she told him. Magic sniffed the air again as the horses in the pasture sized him up. His shiny coat revealed dark dapples on his sides, and his muscles rippled in the sunlight.

The horses felt sure that this new Magic would be a leader among them, and some of the leaders already feared changes that would occur in the hierarchy of the herd. Horses learn to get along together, but they determine an order of which horses are leaders and which follow. So, of course, the leaders were concerned that their places might change with the arrival of this mighty new horse, and some were already planning ways to keep their positions. "He will have to fight with me to get my place," Tara was already saying, and others were quietly agreeing, even though they looked at him with some awe.

The horses were somewhat surprised when they heard Sam saying to this new horse, "Up, Magic! Down!" Why is she saying that? they wondered. What odd things to say! She never said this to other horses.

Sam guided Magic into a stall that was prepared with fresh wood shavings and a flake of timothy hay. "Here you go, boy," she said. "It's okay."

She splashed her hand in his water bucket. Cautiously, Magic moved towards the bucket, then enjoyed a sip of cool water. Next, Sam shuffled her hand in the hay. Again, Magic responded by following the sound of the crackling hay and lowering his head to the food on the floor of his stall. "That's it, Mag! Good boy," Sam said.

The horses knew the routine. It would be several days before this new horse would be turned out with them. Sam always made sure that a new horse felt secure in its new stall before putting him out in the pasture with the rest of the herd. In the meantime, they watched and wondered. Every day, Sam led Magic around places by the barn, saying "Up!" or "Down!" where the area was uneven. What was that about? Magic's former owner, a woman named Jody, also came out and led him around, saying the same words. What could this mean?

In addition, there was activity in the pasture. Volunteers were working on making a small pasture within the larger enclosure. They were pounding posts and nailing beams to portion off a small space. Then they added a "run-in," a space the horses recognized as a place to go to get out of the sun or rain. But why in such a small area, and with no trees for shade?

Chapter Three: Introducing Magic

One day, after the small pasture space was finished, Sam and Jody led Magic into the new enclosure. They walked him around it three times, tapping the fence as they went. Jody stopped at the water trough and splashed the water until Magic lowered his head and drank from the trough.

She walked him into the run-in enclosure and rustled the hay that was placed there. Then she took the halter off of Magic and watched. He stood quietly, but he did not move. After a while, she put his halter on again, and led him through the routine once again. Again, she took off his halter. Magic showed no signs of fear, but again, he did not move.

At this time, of course, all the horses pranced near the small enclosure to get a glimpse of the new horse. Kaycee tried to get close, but he was pushed aside by the leaders of the herd. Finally, he gave up and moved to the far end of the pasture to graze.

As Sam observed this activity, the idea that she had when Magic first arrived grew. "I wonder," she thought. And she decided to give her instinct a try. "What do you think about bringing Mr. K in with Magic?" Sam asked Jody.

"I think it's just what he needs," Jody replied. "He has always done well paired with another horse. At the polo grounds, he was in with eight thoroughbreds, and he navigated the trees in the field just fine. You would never know there was anything different about him. He ran with the herd and rarely had trouble."

"Well, we want to turn that 'rarely' into 'never,'" Sam said. Jody shook her head in agreement. "But I think you're right about a companion. Let me go get Kaycee."

Jody stayed with Magic as Sam walked into the larger field with a lead rope and halter. "Come here, Mr. K!" she called. Kaycee could hardly believe he was being singled out. Was Sam going to put him with that big new horse? He was proud, but afraid. Tara wasn't nearly the size of the new gelding, but she pushed him around all the time. Would this horse named Magic hurt him?

"Hi, Mr. K. Time to meet Magic!" Sam said as she slipped the halter over Kaycee's head. He was nervous, but he had always been able to trust Sam to take care of him, so he walked willingly with her into the small paddock.

Magic turned as Sam and Kaycee entered his paddock, and he called in greeting. Kaycee whinnied back.

"Good boy!" Sam reassured Kaycee, and she slowly led him towards Magic and Jody, stopping short by about six feet. Next, Sam and Jody brought the two horses nose to nose. Okay, Sam thought to herself. This is where I have to trust my sense and horse sense. Sam slipped the halter off of Kaycee's head and watched. Jody backed away to stand with Sam. Because he had often been kicked and bitten as the lowest horse in the group, Kaycee was wary. He noticed, though, that Magic made no attempt to bite or kick him. Slowly, Kaycee's confidence grew, and he finally came close enough to reach out to Magic's nose to share a breath of air with him. To Kaycee's surprise, Magic let out a long breath of relief. Could he have found a friend?

Kaycee stepped in closer. Only then he noticed something disturbingly different about his potential new friend. Magic did not have any eyes! Kaycee had never seen anything like this! How could a horse survive without eyes? At first, he backed up, and he thought about pushing Magic with his teeth and legs as he had been pushed around by the other horses. After all, Magic would not see it coming. Then he thought about how he felt when he was bullied this way and how sad it made him. He decided he would not be so unkind.

Kaycee did not know if he could talk to his new pasture mate about his difference or not. He stayed near Magic and shared flakes of hay with him quietly, trying to sense what he might say. Finally, he braved the question, "Why do you not have eyes?"

Magic stopped eating hay. After a moment, he responded, "So you have eyes?"

"Of course I do," Kaycee replied. "What happened to yours?"

Magic was curious. "Oh, now things are making more sense! I guessed it wasn't common for a horse to be blind. But I never knew for sure. Am I the only horse you have ever met who doesn't have eyes?"

"Yes, of course! In fact, I've never heard of a horse without eyes. Have you always been without them?" Kaycee asked.

"No, I was born with eyes, and I could see until I was six years old, though I lost the sight in one eye when I was five. I'm fourteen now. Humans were always talking about me being different because I was blind, but no horse before you ever talked to me about it – well, except my best friend, Zan. I wonder why?" Magic said.

Kaycee replied, "Well, horses here will surely ask you about it. We get to work with children that some humans say are 'different.' Some need a wheelchair to get around when they're not riding a horse. Some have difficulty controlling their muscles. Some don't know as many words as others. Honestly, I think we horses have lots more sense than humans. As we see it, there are two kinds of humans: ones that are nice to us, and ones that are not. Our riders here are wonderful to us! Maybe the horses you lived with before you were here never got to know kids like our riders. So maybe they didn't know how to talk to you about your blindness."

Kaycee hung his head. "Still, I'm sorry. What a terrible thing to happen to you."

Magic sensed Kaycee's pity. "Oh, no. Don't feel sorry for me! I am fortunate. If I had another owner, I might not be alive today. As it is, I'm more comfortable since I had my eyes removed, and I'm happy to have this new life where I can help the children who ride here. If you'll stay with me, I'll tell you my story."

Kaycee swished flies off of Magic's back with his tail. "Really? You want *me* to stay with you? Me? The other horses are afraid of you! You promise you won't kick me or bite me? I'm not the grandest horse in the field. I am old and gray. But if you let me be your companion, I'd be happy to help you find the water trough and our piles of hay."

Magic replied, "Kaycee, I've also been the horse that was bullied, kicked, and bitten. I don't see your age or your gray hairs. They don't matter to me. If I could see them, I would think of the silver-grey hairs as shiny reminders of the wisdom that comes with age. Thanks for offering to be my friend!"

Kaycee said, "Will you tell me how you lost your eyes?"

Magic responded, "Yes, my new friend, I will. But today has been filled with adventures, and I'm tired. Let's save it for tomorrow…"

Sam and Jody watched the two geldings sharing hay in the run-in for about a half hour and felt satisfied that the idea was a good one. Then they saw Kaycee start to walk away from Magic. "I wonder if there's a problem," Sam said.

"No. I've seen this before. Just watch," Jody replied.

After taking several steps away, Kaycee turned back towards Magic. Magic stood still. Mr. K walked back to Magic, then away again. Then he neighed to Magic. Magic began to walk towards Kaycee. Kaycee took more steps away and whinnied again. This process continued until Kaycee was able to lead Magic to the water trough at the end of the paddock.

"That's amazing!" Sam said. "How could he know to do that?"

"I think there are so many things we don't know about horses' intelligence," Jody replied. "I've ridden Magic through new places and he just 'knew' when we were coming up to things that might block his way. I remember him skirting wide around a junk washer that someone had put at the side of a road to be picked up as trash. I've ridden many horses in my life, and Magic is as safe as any sighted horse I've ridden, and safer than some. I know he will do just fine in his new life here."

Chapter Four: Magic's Story – The Early Years

Thunderstorms announced the next morning, so Magic and Kaycee chose to spend their time under the run-in shed. The other horses had not had the chance to meet Magic up close, so they were curious both about him and about the fact that Kaycee had been chosen to be his companion. How could this dull, old horse be chosen as a companion to the shiny new gelding?

Kaycee led Magic to the hay flakes in the shed that they shared during the day. "Please," he said, "I want to know your story. I've never met another blind horse."

"It's a long story," Magic responded. "But it's a stormy day, so a good time to start my tale, if you really want to hear it."

"Yes, please!" Kaycee said. "Also," he said, "I see that you are not only blind, but that you have a large scar on your right hip. Are the two related?"

So Magic began.

"I'm fourteen now. My first memories are from the age of two. I didn't really belong to anybody. When people came, I was afraid. One day, a group of men yelled and scared us to race around the pasture. I ended up pressed against the barbed wired fence. No one seemed to care until the cut didn't stop bleeding. Finally, someone called a vet. He was angry that I had not been treated hours before, as the cut was over a foot long. He stitched the cut. Jody told me that it isn't ugly. She says that no one could steal me, as she could always recognize me by this cut. Maybe that was the beginning of good luck I've had."

Kaycee raised his head at the mention of Jody. "I've met your Jody, too, and she always gives me treats. Who is she, and how did you find her?" he asked.

Magic took a long munch of hay before he answered. "As I remember it, a new horse came to our barn in Georgia. Then a young girl named Katie came to ride him every day, and her mother came to watch. That was Jody. I had arrived at that barn just a few weeks before them, and I had never been ridden. The man who owned the barn bought me at an auction – I feel sure that if he had not, that I might've gone to a terrible place."

"Anyway, Jody used to own horses and compete them in horse shows. She asked if there were any horses that needed work so that she could ride with her daughter, Katie. The owner offered me. I was afraid! The people I lived with before used to hit me, and I was afraid of having anyone touch my head. The other horses in the pasture were stronger than I, so I didn't get much to eat, and my ribs showed through my barrel. My coat was dull and covered with bite marks. I had never had a saddle on my back, and I was afraid I'd make mistakes. I remember Jody saying that I couldn't walk a straight line when she first began to ride me."

I was afraid of being hurt again, but Jody kept riding me and she never hurt me as I learned to do what she asked. One day, the farmer that owned me brought people out who wanted to buy me. I was sad that I wouldn't see Jody again. The next thing I knew, Jody was my owner, and she secured me a stall in the barn where I could always eat grain without fighting for it among the other horses in the field. Jody added beet pulp to my diet to help me gain weight. In a few months, my ribs were covered and my coat was shiny. No one could believe the change in me!"

"There was, though, something that no one could change. Usually when humans buy a horse they first have what they call a 'vet check' to be sure the horse is physically sound. When I was checked, I had a bad eye infection. It was what brought me to lose my sight, something called 'equine euveitis.' At that time, my right eye looked cloudy and white. The vet told Jody that there were lots of bugs around that summer and that I was probably reacting to problems with insects. Since that time, Jody has said to me lots of times that she is glad the vet didn't know what was wrong, as she might not have bought me. I don't think I'd still be alive if she did not, as vets at a university told her to put me down if I went blind. I didn't really know what that meant. For some reason, Jody believed that I would be safe even when I lost my sight. I guess I'm not what anyone would consider to be a 'normal' horse, but that's pretty silly, isn't it? I can carry any rider on my back and do what I am asked."

Kaycee reflected on Magic's words and on the goals of the farm. It was named SMART, the Sarasota Manatee Association for Riding Therapy, and its riders came with numerous special needs and challenges. Kaycee had seen many children gain confidence as they learned to ride horses hundreds of pounds larger than they. He could not imagine how a blind horse could safely carry a rider. He liked Magic and was so much happier now that he was always pastured with him. Still, Kaycee led Magic to the water and to the piles of hay that were scattered in their paddock. How could he do the work of a SMART horse?

Chapter Five: A Morning Workout

The next morning, Jody arrived early at the barn, about an hour after the horses had their morning grain. She swung open her car door and called, "Hi, Mag!" and Magic turned his head towards her, as though he were looking at her. "Want some cookies?"

Magic nickered. "Cookies" was their code word for any of his favorite crunchy treats – apples, carrots, or a special brand of horse snack that Jody bought at the local tack store.

Kaycee whinnied, too. "Oh, of course, Mr. K! I wouldn't forget you!" Kaycee decided he had even more good reason to be picked as Magic's companion, if Jody was going to give him treats, too!

Jody and Sam exchanged greetings and chatted about the hot summer weather. Then Jody put Magic's halter on and led him away from his paddock. "Ok, boy, you've had time to adjust. It's time to get back to work," she said. Jody led him to a hitching post where she had placed his grooming box, saddle, pads, and bridle. Kaycee watched as she curried and brushed Magic's shiny bay coat and black mane and tail. She carefully picked out his feet and gently rubbed a damp cloth on his face and in his eye sockets.

Then she fit his saddle on his back and slowly tightened the girth. After she took off his halter, she took several minutes to rub Magic's face and ears. He pressed his face against her body in a kind of hug. Then she took the bridle, and Magic opened his mouth to accept the bit. "She's really going to ride him!" Kaycee thought. "I can't believe this!"

Jody led Magic to the mounting area that the SMART riders used. Sam had asked her to get Magic ready for the routine he would have once the riders returned from their summer break. Jody tapped on the wood to let Magic know there was a structure there. He stopped quietly while she adjusted her stirrups. Then she mounted him, took the reins, and said, "Walk on, Mag." And off he walked, no different than any sighted horse!

When they got to a bump or depression in the ground, Jody would say, "Up," or "Down, Mag." Kaycee noticed that the one time she forgot to say this, Magic stumbled a bit. Jody walked him into the fenced-in riding ring and walked around it once. Then she said, "Trot, Magic!" Again, Kaycee was amazed that Magic would have the courage to move so quickly when he could not see where he was going. Kaycee even tried to close his eyes and trot a few steps himself, but he found it scary. So he was really amazed when Jody said, "Canter!" and Magic took off at an even faster speed. The pair not only went around the arena; they also did circles, loops, diagonals and serpentines. Kaycee saw Magic shorten and lengthen his strides and perform leg yields, a sideways movement that dressage horses are taught to do at the trot.

After the practice in the arena, Jody took Magic out into the large field and walked him through trees – and over logs. She would stop him just before a log and say "Up, up, up!" That would make Magic raise his legs high to walk over the log. Kaycee could hardly believe this was happening. He knew he had to learn more about this unusual horse. That morning he came to believe that Magic had certainly earned his name. What he was doing seemed magical to Kaycee.

Chapter Six: Show Days

After the workout, Jody brought Magic to the wash stall and gave him a bath. She toweled him dry and returned him to his paddock where she split an apple between Kaycee and Magic. "OK, guys, see you next week," she said. "You be good for Sam, Mag. She takes great care of you." Magic pointed his head towards Jody as she walked off, then towards the truck as it rattled down the gravel drive. "A whole week!" he said. "That's a long time."

Kaycee swished at some flies with his tail. "I'm sorry," he said. "I can tell you miss her. Sam said something about her new job taking lots of time."

"I know," Magic replied. "That's why she looked for a new home where I would get lots of attention and get ridden often. But when Jody first bought me, she was able to come see me almost every day. And then there were the days when she kept me in a barn right at her house and took care of me every day! For three of those years, I could still see. And she took me to dressage shows and horse trials. Then dressage shows even after I lost my sight. It was fun."

Kaycee reached for some hay left from the morning feeding. "I've been in SMART horse shows, but I don't know what you mean by dressage and horse trials. Please tell me more of your story."

So Magic began.

"I told you that I hadn't been ridden before Jody came along. She and her daughter Katie took turns training me. Jody talked a lot about something called 'dressage.' It's a training method that, when done right, lets horses move the way we do in the wild. Of course, humans aren't very good at it, and it takes them a long time to understand how to let us move that way. I think it is more training for people than for horses, even though they seem to think it's the other way around. When done right, it teaches people how to let horses balance ourselves from our hindquarters so that we are light in the front. That lets us perform some fancy moves sideways or in circles. I've heard Jody call them terms like 'half pass' and 'pirouette.'"

"I never got that far, though. There are lots of levels in dressage, starting at training level, then first to fourth level, then four more international levels, with the top one called 'grand prix.' I showed at first level and trained at second. That means I learned a few different ways to move in walk, trot, and canter, and I can trot sideways in a move Jody calls a 'leg yield.'"

"Well, I'm impressed," said Kaycee. "I've never heard anything about this before. But I did see you moving sideways and stretching out your trot and walk when Jody was riding you. Is that what you're talking about?"

"Yes," Magic replied. "Jody's daughter Katie, though, was more interested in jumping. She taught me how to leap over logs and wooden fences after I turned four. And when I was five, she took me to special shows called "events" or 'horse trials.' There she competed me in dressage and something called 'cross country,' where we would run through fields and over all kinds of jumps and through water. That was fun! And the final phase was called 'stadium jumping,' where we would jump over a number of jumps in an arena. I think the cross country was my favorite. I got to run and run between jumps, and I had lots of time between jumps, so I could set myself up to make it over them easily. The stadium jumps would fall down if you touched them with a hoof, and the turns were tight, so there wasn't much space between them. Those made me a little nervous. But I always tried my best. I remember my first horse trial. There were 25 horses in my division. Just like dressage, there are many levels, depending on how long you've been working at it and how advanced you were. Most horses are at the lower levels, as was I. I came in second out of 25 in my first horse trial!"

"It all sounds so exciting," Kaycee said. "I wish I could see what it's like. I've never jumped anything! Is it hard?"

Magic thought for a moment. "I used to jump things in my pasture just for fun. That was without a rider, though. It's really only hard when the rider doesn't take you in front of the jump well. Katie was good at it. Jody wasn't as good, but I think that's why she preferred dressage. She never asked me to jump anything big, so it worked out okay."

"Do you still jump?" Kaycee asked.

"Oh, goodness, no! I can easily follow a rider's signals on the ground, but I could never know how high or wide to jump without being able to see!" Magic responded.

"I saw how well you and Jody worked this morning, and I wondered how you could do that," said Mr. K. "To be honest, I tried closing my eyes and trotting in our field, and I was afraid. How do you do what you do?"

"Oh, that's another story," said Magic. "Right now I want to take a nap in the sun. Tomorrow, maybe?"

"Deal," said Kaycee, and they both found a space to stretch out for a rest until Sam called them in for their evening grain.

Chapter Seven: SMART Riders

The next day was a big one: the SMART riders were returning after a summer break! Sam and other volunteers were busy all day getting the horses ready to see the riders again. They took turns being bathed and groomed. Sam was there all day talking to the horses about their jobs that afternoon when the riders arrived.

After their baths, Magic and Mr. K went to their paddock to relax and enjoy some hay before the afternoon activities. Kaycee was surprised that Magic did not seem worried.

"Aren't you nervous?" he asked Magic. "There will be lots of children, and they will all gather around to see you. You can't see them. Doesn't that make you afraid?"

Magic finished chewing on some grain. Then he said to Kaycee, "I've always loved children. They have never been mean to me like some adults have been. Just like you said to me, there seem to be two kinds of humans: those who are kind to us, and those who are mean. The children I've known have always been kind. There were always children at the barn when Jody first became my owner. When she moved me to her own house, she used to bring groups of children there to have picnics, swim in her pool, and ride me. She worked as their summer camp counselor. Even after I had surgery to remove my eyes, they came and rode me. They all wanted to pet me and hug me and ride me. I guess that's why I didn't think that there was anything so unusual about me. I came to look forward to the running and loud squeals of the children who had never been on a horse before. Do you think the SMART riders will be like those children?" Magic asked.

If horses could smile, that is what Kaycee would have done. "SMART riders are the best!" he said. "I wish you could see them. I wish you could see their smiles. Sam has told me that many of our riders have difficult lives and that not all humans treat them like they would treat Sam or your Jody, just because they may have trouble walking or talking or understanding some things. Maybe it's a bit like our world. You know, before you were here, a couple of the other horses would kick and bite me because I am small and getting gray. I was afraid you would do that, too. And then, when I saw that you did not have eyes, just for a moment I thought of treating you that way, just because I could. It was what I was used to. But then I thought, why would I do to you what made me sad? I'm glad I didn't behave that way. Magic, I'm so glad you're my friend."

Magic swished his tail to pick a fly off of Kaycee's back. "SMART riders sound great!" he said. "And maybe people and horses aren't so different. I told you about the humans around me before I met Jody. They weren't so nice. Neither were some of the horses I was with before she separated me from them so I could eat my own grain and get strong. I'm glad you're my friend too, Kaycee."

Cars began to bounce down the rutted gravel road towards the stables. "SMART riders!" Kaycee whinnied. A volunteer brought Kaycee and Magic to their stalls so that the riders could greet them. The children walked excitedly by the horses with the help of volunteers. Most of them knew Mr. K and the other horses, and they were happy to pat them after their long summer break. Sam led small groups to meet Magic. "This is our new horse, Magic," she said. Mag lowered his head to where he sensed the children were, so that they could pet his face and neck. The SMART riders were saying things like "He's beautiful!" and "Can I ride him?" After a while, one rider said, "Where are his eyes?"

Sam said, "Magic's eyes stopped working many years ago, but because of a disease, they hurt him even after he went blind. So his owner asked the horse doctor if she would take them out so he would feel better. And because he is such a 'SMART' horse, he can be ridden without eyes! So what do you think of that?"

The children reached to pet him and said, "I want to ride him!"

Jody walked towards the children and Sam. "Glad you could make it," said Sam. Then she said to the riders, "You know we always need to train our horses to know what to do first. Jody owned Magic before he became a SMART horse, and she trained him. So she will ride him in your lessons until we know he's ready for you. Don't worry! You'll get to ride him soon!"

Jody saddled Magic and joined the group of riders. This was the first time he was in the same area with the other SMART horses. They had been gossiping about him for several weeks and were pleased to finally have a chance to meet him close up. Of course, they all wanted to ask the same questions that Kaycee had. Magic had come to understand from Kaycee that he was unusual. Patiently, he said, "I'll tell you all about it, another day."

Chapter Eight: Going Blind

Over breakfast the next day, Kaycee said, "Okay, Magic. You told me you would explain how you can get around without eyes. I watched you yesterday when you knew where to put your head so that the SMART riders could pet you, and I've watched you as Jody rides you through the fields. How do you do this?"

"Two things," Magic replied. "Trust and training. After Jody came to own me, my eyes kept getting infections. They would get runny or cloudy. Sometimes I'd wrinkle up my face because they were so painful, and sometimes I'd have to close my eyes and would not feel much like being ridden. Jody had the vet look at them lots when I would get like this. They could see that my sight was getting worse. Just before I turned six years old, the vet told Jody that my left eye stopped working. Then when Jody rode me, she started to do things like raise my reins a little bit and say "Up!" when we would go up a hill or over a log, and "Down!" when we would go down a hill. After a while, I knew what to expect when she did these things.

One beautiful fall evening – I remember it so well, because it is the last day I ever saw – Jody was riding me with her daughter Katie on her horse, Paddington. They decided to gallop up a long hill together. Halfway up that hill, the little sight I had remaining in my right eye seemed like it was swallowed up like a sunset. I couldn't see! I panicked and started to buck. I still feel bad about it. Jody was thrown to the ground, and I continued to gallop up the hill. I heard Jody crying out, "Magic!" Finally I stopped. Katie jumped off Paddington and caught me. We waited for what seemed like such a long time for Jody to get up and walk up the hill. I could feel her moving her hands quickly towards my right eye, but I couldn't see a thing. I guess I didn't blink. I remember Jody saying, "He's blind," and throwing her arms around me, crying into my neck. I wasn't afraid anymore. I knew she was there, and I knew she would take care of me.

Jody walked me back to the barn, using those words and movements with the bridle that she had been teaching me: "Up!" "Down."

"What a story! Weren't you scared? Were you angry?" Kaycee asked.

"I don't remember everything I felt," Magic said "As I think back on it, I should have been afraid. Remember, I told you that Jody took me to a veterinary school at a university after I lost the sight in my left eye to see if they could save my right eye. They told her no and that she should put me down if I went blind, because I would not be safe."

"But she didn't!" Kaycee said.

"No, she decided they were wrong," Magic replied. "Humans live and do wonderful things without sight, without hearing, without legs. They just need someone to believe in them. Jody believed in me. And so, I had to trust her."

"I had one other who trusted me. There was another horse in the field, the best friend I ever had. Her name was Zan. Jody and Katie used to call us 'Romeo and Juliet.' I'm not sure what that means, but I guessed it had to do with being best friends. And Zan was my best friend. That very first week that I couldn't see was scary. But Zan never left my side. I could always feel her next to me. I got tired quickly at first, because it took so much energy for me to walk around without knowing where I was. Often I would lie down to take a nap. Whenever I woke up, Zan would be standing over me.

Katie's horse Paddington was my other friend. He used to race around the pasture with me. Sometimes, as we were galloping in a big circle, he would kick at me, and that would make me run in a circle just inside his circle. I didn't understand it at the time. Since I've had time to think about it, though, I think he did that to keep me from running into the fence."

"I've never had such a good friend," Kaycee said. Then he added, "Except for now."

"Thanks," Magic replied. "You're a great friend, too.

"A week after I went blind, I heard Jody coming into the pasture. She came up to me and lay things on the ground. Then she started the routine we had for the years before I went blind. She brushed me and picked out my feet. Then she placed her saddle on my back and bridled me. The next thing I knew, she led me out of the pasture and placed herself gently on my back, saying, "Ok. Walk on, Magic."

"The last time she was on you, you threw her off! What did you do?" asked Mr. K.

"Oh, I remembered that all too well," said Magic. "It was the last thing I wanted to do again. So, I did what I was trained to do. I walked on. There were steep hills where we lived, so I really paid attention when she said, 'Up!' or 'Down!' After a while, I got comfortable and remembered how much I loved to have Jody ride me. Then she said, 'Trot, Magic!' Before I could think about it, I was trotting. I was so used to trotting when Jody said 'trot'! And then, I knew. I could do this. I would be okay. I had a human I could trust. When I could see, Jody had never put me in danger. Why would she do that now? Of course she would not. And so, that was a new beginning for me. I couldn't see, but Jody saw for me."

Chapter Nine: Show Days

Magic was becoming accustomed to SMART riders on his back for weekly lessons. He had always loved children, so he was usually patient as they were asked to stand quietly before trying tasks such as stopping by mailboxes to open the box and pull out an object or walking onto a wooden platform and standing quietly before moving on. Sometimes, though, he had a hard time standing still, and he needed to be trained to stand for longer periods of time than he was used to.

Kaycee asked Magic, "Why do you always want to walk on?"

Magic explained, "Remember, I was trained to be a show horse, then an event horse."

"What does that mean?" asked Mr. K.

"They're not too different," said Magic. "Show horses move through walk, trot, canter, or they go over a series of jumps, as soon as they are in the show ring. In event, you aren't called to do anything until you are told to move – either in a dressage test, or going through a field of jumps, or in a ring where jumps are set up," he said. There is a little bit of standing around while you wait for your number to be called. But Jody could always tell if I was feeling nervous, and she would let me walk around before it was my turn to perform. Now, I just need to get over feeling nervous when I need to stand still. I can do it! The riders here are so kind. I just need to practice."

"I know you can, and I have heard the SMART riders say how much they want to ride you," said Kaycee. "I was just wondering – did you do anything between all of your showing and coming to SMART?"

"I did," Magic said. "As I told you, Jody bought me in Georgia. But then she got a job in Florida. By that time, I was blind. She didn't have her own horse trailer, so she had to hire someone to bring me to Florida. And before she got me here, she had to convince someone who had never heard of a blind horse to board me in their pasture."

"I know you now, Magic, but I have to say that I can't imagine another human giving you that chance. Here, at SMART, yes. But anywhere else? You must tell me who!"

"Jody had been reading the classified notices for boarding horses in this area. She called a woman, Barb, who seemed to be taken by my story, and she said she would give it a chance. Jody was there when the trailer arrived. Barb watched as Jody walked me off the trailer. She thought I should just be in a stall for a few days, but Jody told her that I would do better if I knew where I was. Really, it wasn't much different than going to a horse show or event. Right away, she saddled me and rode me through the field. Of course, I could tell when we were heading for a group of trees, and I would slow down to go through them. Barb was so surprised! Barb had a pony that she thought would make a good pasture mate for me. Jesse and I became good friends."

"I stayed there for about six months and was happy, but it was far for Jody to visit, so she checked to see if there were any boarding spots at the local polo fields. She found one man, a polo player from South Africa, who was willing to give me a chance. There were all kinds of rules at the polo community, and Jody could only ride me off his property if she was with him and his polo ponies. Soon we were cantering around the polo track three times every week with Stuart and his friends. Many of the polo trainers were Spanish speaking. I remember what they said so well, before they got to know me. As they would canter past me, they would turn around to say, "Hola" (hello). Then they would see my face, and cry out, "¡Él no tiene ojos! ¿Qué pasó?" That's Spanish for, "He doesn't have any eyes! What happened?" They came to learn my story, and we were all friends.

"That sounds like a good place to be," said Mr. K. "So what brought you here?"

"I remember Jody coming to me and putting her arms around my neck," said Magic. She had to take a job that made her work many hours, and she told me she couldn't ride me as much as she had always ridden me. She said she found me a home where I would be well loved and where she would still be able to ride me every week, even though she wouldn't have the same time to come and ride as often as she had always ridden me.

"Of course, I was sad. In Georgia, I had lived on her land, and she had cared for me every day. When we moved to Florida, I saw her three or four times every week. And now she was telling me that she would only see me once every week. Jody was the only owner I had ever had. I was sad and afraid."

"But then I met Sam. And I met you. And I met the SMART riders. SMART riders don't judge me because I don't have eyes. I can carry them through competitions! And we can care for each other. And, of course, I get to see Jody every week. So I am content."

Chapter Ten: A SMART Competition

Fall days had turned to short days of winter, and Magic became used to his new routine. SMART riders came on Tuesday and Thursday evenings and on Saturday mornings. Jody came on Friday mornings. Sam and Gail and other SMART volunteers took care of all the horses every morning and evening. And Magic spent every day with Kaycee. They became great friends. Magic no longer needed a guide to the water trough or the run-in shed, but the two horses would follow one another just to have the companionship.

Magic got better at standing still during lessons. Volunteers led him when SMART riders rode him. Sometimes they walked onto wooden bridges or zigzagged between cones. At other times they walked into a small ditch or up and over a small hill. At those times, the SMART riders learned to say "Up!" and "Down, Magic!" just as Jody had taught them.

There were other obstacles that staff thought might bother Magic, but Jody would lead him through them, and he trusted that she would not put him in a situation that would hurt him.

Magic loved the riders and the time he spent with the other horses during lessons. Even Kaycee had become more confident among the other horses, and the ones that used to pick on him became friendly. They decided there must be something special about Mr. K for him to be chosen to spend his days with this unusual horse that could safely canter around his field when he was feeling cold or frisky, even though he could not see.

One February evening, Sam brought the riders and horses together before the lesson. "Okay, SMART riders," she said. "This is the time of year when we get ready for our spring competition!"

Magic perked up his ears when he heard that word, "competition." Could it be another horse show? Magic always loved shows. When Jody showed him, she would always bathe him and brush him until his coat was soft and shiny. She always rubbed his saddle and bridle with a pleasant smelling oil. Most of the horses at the shows were proud to be carrying their riders into the ring where they would do their best to be noticed by the judge. They were happy times.

The SMART riders seemed to feel the same way about shows. When Sam said that word, they began to cheer and talk about how they would practice and do their best. The riders and their leaders also practiced a drill team exercise to music. They would pair up, side by side, and walk up the middle of the ring, then split apart and do circles, coming back together at the center.

Magic and Kaycee were contentedly munching on breakfast hay the next morning. Magic said, "I'm so happy to be ridden to music again! When Jody competed me in dressage, that was our favorite part of the competition. She said it was called 'kur,' or 'musical freestyle.' Jody would make up a routine to fit the music. She would find music that matched the speed of my walk, trot, and canter."

"I like being ridden to music, too," said Kaycee. It has such a happy sound."

Jody didn't get to the SMART lessons very often, because she was often at work, but she was there when the riders practiced to music one evening. It reminded her of how much she loved to ride to music. The next Friday morning, she brought her CD player when she came to ride, and some of the music she used when she competed Magic. She finished her practice with a big smile on her face. Magic pranced to the music in a way that Sam had not seen him move before.

"What would you think of riding Magic to music for a performance at the SMART show?" Sam asked Jody. "The kids love him, and the parents know how good he is when he has a lead by his side. But most of them don't know that he can be ridden like this, trotting and cantering in patterns around the ring. I think people would love to see what he can do."

Jody thought for a minute. "We're sure not as good as we used to be when I could ride Mag every day," she said. But if we keep it simple, sure, it would be fun. I'll look for something special for music, and we'll dedicate it to the SMART riders."

When Jody drove away from the farm that morning, she thought about the music she had used in the past. Their favorite freestyle music had been a fun collection of swing music, but Jody thought that would be too fast for them now that they didn't practice so much. She was listening to one of her favorite CDs in her truck as she was thinking.

Then she paused to listen, and she smiled. Yes, this was the perfect piece. It had a slow start, and it built up in the middle and quieted down at the end. And the words – there could be none better. When she got home, Jody got to work on a routine that would match the music.

The SMART horse competition was just a week away when Jody brought the music out and practiced on a Friday morning. Sam had been cleaning the stalls, but she stopped to watch when she heard the music come on. When Magic trotted up to her at the end of the song, Sam was wiping tears from her eyes. "That is beautiful," she said. "The kids are going to love it."

"It's perfect, isn't it?" said Jody. "For Magic, for the SMART riders and other riders that will compete next Saturday. Thanks for asking us to do this ride. We both feel honored, me most of all. I am so grateful that you took a chance on Magic to let him come here and have a new home."

During the week, Sam and the other volunteers came to the farm to bathe the horses and clean their tack. The morning of the show was a typically warm and sunny Florida day. Magic would be taking three SMART riders into classes in the competition. First, though, he had his special performance.

Kaycee was also clean and shiny from his bath, and his long golden mane looked like silk. He was excited to be in the competition. "How do you feel?" he asked Magic.

"Excited. Nervous. I want to do my best for my SMART riders. And I don't want to make mistakes during Jody's musical ride."

"Don't worry," said Mr. K. "I've been watching Jody and you practice. You'll do a great job, I know."

"Thanks," said Magic. "It is important to me. You know, I've done many things in my life, but being at this farm and working with SMART riders has been the best of all for me. I want to help them feel proud of all they have learned to do."

Just then, the loudspeaker came on. Gail was the speaker. "We will be starting in just five minutes, everyone. Make your final preparations, and enjoy the show!"

Jody came to Magic. "I guess that means it's time for me to get on you, boy," she said, as she gave Kaycee a pat. "See you later, Mr. K!"

Kaycee whinnied as the two rode away. Jody took Magic into a practice field and put him into a trot, then a canter. "Good boy!" she said. "You feel great today! Let's go ride for SMART!"

They walked back towards the main ring, and Gail spoke again. "Before we begin the show classes, we have a special treat. SMART riders and families have come to know our new horse Magic, but those of you who trailered in for the competition do not. You may not have noticed, but Magic does not have any eyes. He's been blind for six years, over half of his life. He is here to prove about horses what you already know about people. It doesn't matter what the challenge is that you may face – whether you are blind or can't hear or have a leg that you can't move. What matters is that we all try and do our best and that we never give up. Here is Magic to show you what he can do because he didn't give up. His rider, Jody, wants to dedicate this ride to all of you competitors for your hard work and training that brought you to compete today. Good luck to all!"

Riders and spectators cheered as Magic charged powerfully across the ring's diagonal to the words of a popular song:

Don't give up

Because you want to be heard…

Don't give up

Because you want to burn bright;

If darkness blinds you,

I will shine to guide you.

Everybody wants to be understood;

Well, I can hear you.

Everybody wants to be loved;

Don't give up,

Because you are loved.

(lyrics from "You Are Loved," by Josh Groban)

As Magic and Jody came to a halt at the center of the ring with the last beat of the music, Magic heard their clapping and cheers. Jody patted Magic's shiny neck and smiled. "It looks like you're home, Mag," she said.

The End

CPSIA information can be obtained at www.ICGtesting.com
Printed in the USA
LVIW01n1929140317
527169LV00003B/18